TENNIS ACE

The #1 Sports Writer for Kids

TENNIS ACE

Little, Brown and Company
Boston   New York   London

First Edition

Library of Congress Cataloging-in-Publication Data

Christopher, Matt.
    Tennis ace / Matt Christopher. — 1st ed.
        p.   cm.   *II-ω—υπε*
    Summary: Steve and Ginny are frustrated because their father ig-
nores her talent as a tennis player while pushing him harder and
harder to win at the sport.
    ISBN 0-316-13519-4 (hc) — ISBN 0-316-13491-0 (pb)
    [1. Tennis — Fiction.   2. Parent and child — Fiction.
3. Brothers and sisters — Fiction.]   I. Title.
PZ7.C458Th   2000
[Fic] — dc21   99-048067

10 9 8 7 6 5 4 3 2 1

MV-NY

Printed in the United States of America

To Julia Catherine

TENNIS ACE

1

Steve Greeley wiped his face with a towel. His throat was dry, and he wished he had a gallon of cold water or lemonade right now. He felt exhausted . . . and all he was doing was sitting in the bleachers, watching his sister Ginny play a tennis match. It was an awesomely steamy day.

Ginny, who was fourteen, was playing a quarterfinal in the girls' fourteen-and-under class of the State Junior Tennis Championship. She didn't seem to mind the heat at all. Ginny had amazing stamina, and at the moment she was running her opponent, a tall, slender girl, back and forth across the baseline with perfectly placed forehands. Ginny looked cool and in control. Steve, twelve, was due to play his own match in a few minutes: a quarterfinal in the boys' twelve-and-under class. He was hot and uncomfortable enough for both of them.

Next to him, his father nudged him with an elbow. "I used to love playing on days like this," Mr. Greeley said. "I'd make my opponents run around until they were ready to drop, just like Ginny's doing to that poor kid now."

Ted Greeley had been the star of his college tennis team when he was younger. In fact, as both his kids knew, he had been considered a good prospect for the pro tour. He believed that he might have gone on to have a great career and become a household name, but a knee injury had put an end to his dreams of stardom. He had made it clear he wanted to see his son accomplish what he hadn't been able to do.

Steve shrugged. "I won't have to work that hard today. I'm playing Charlie Silver, and I beat him twice already this year."

Mr. Greeley frowned at his son. "Don't take Charlie for granted. He'll be psyched up today. He'll go all out to win, and you'd better plan on doing the same thing."

Steve wiped his face again. "I'll take care of Charlie, don't worry. I have to pace myself, that's all. The semis are tomorrow, and it could be just as hot."

Ginny smashed a cross-court forehand just out of her opponent's reach, and the crowd applauded.

"Game to Miss Greeley," the umpire announced. "She leads the first set, five games to two."

Mr. Greeley clapped, too, but he was studying his son and looking anxious. "It's important that you play your best today. I don't want you to just get by. You should dominate this match."

Steve stared at his father. "Huh? How come today is so important? It's not the finals."

"Well," said his father, "there's a special reason, but it's a surprise. You'll find out after your match. For now, you'll have to trust me that you'll really be happy about it. But you should give it all you've got, believe me. Okay?"

"Sure." Steve didn't feel like arguing. He knew that he could beat Charlie. He wondered why his dad was being so mysterious. Maybe Dad was going to give him the CD player he'd been wanting, as a reward for doing well. He decided that there wasn't any point in thinking about it now and turned his attention to the court below, where Ginny was about to serve for what could be the game that won the set.

Ginny had been perfecting a topspin serve that

jumped away from an opponent, and she used it now. Sure enough, the ball hit the corner of the service box, then darted away like a startled rabbit.

The other player seemed to know that she was beaten. Clearly she was feeling the heat, even though Ginny might as well have been playing on a cool day in Alaska, for all the weather seemed to affect her.

Steve sometimes wished that he had his sister's steely determination and her ability to focus completely on tennis. On the other hand, he liked his life the way it was. Tennis was fun, but there was so much else to enjoy: good music, movies, hanging out with his friends . . .

His father cut off his train of thought with a tap on his arm. "Let's go. You have to get ready for your match."

"*Now?*" Steve pointed to the clock on the clubhouse wall. "I have lots of time. We can watch Ginny for a while yet."

"You need to warm up," his dad insisted.

"In this weather?" Steve started to laugh, but the laughter died in his throat when he saw his father's expression.

Mr. Greeley stood up. "I know you, Champ. You

need a lot of time to get your head into the game. Don't worry about Ginny; she's got this match all sewn up and she doesn't need us to sit here rooting for her. She'll understand that you have your own worries to deal with. Let's go."

Steve knew that there was no point in trying to change his dad's mind once it was set. He sighed and followed his father as they edged their way to the aisle.

On the court, Ginny looked up and caught her brother's eye. She frowned. Steve shrugged and pointed to their father.

Ginny smiled, letting Steve know she knew why they were leaving. Steve gave her a thumbs-up sign.

As they headed toward the clubhouse, Steve heard the solid *thwack* of Ginny's serve and applause from the crowd. The umpire said, "Thirty–love."

Her match would be over in seconds. They could easily have stayed to see her win. It didn't seem fair to Steve. But that's the way it was.

You just didn't argue with Ted Greeley when it came to tennis.

2

When Steve and his dad entered the club locker room, there were only a couple of men at one end. Charlie Silver, Steve noted, was nowhere in sight yet. Apparently, *Charlie* didn't need that much time to "get his head into the game." But Steve kept his thoughts to himself. He wondered again what his dad's surprise might be and went to get a drink of water from the fountain at the end of the room.

"Don't drink too much," cautioned Mr. Greeley. "You don't want to get bloated."

Steve, who had known that without being told, straightened up and smiled at his father. "I sure don't," he said.

Mr. Greeley sat on a bench and stared hard at

6

Steve. "You remember your other matches against Charlie?" he asked. "What were his weaknesses?"

Steve, who had been through this kind of grilling before, was careful not to show his impatience. And who knew, maybe it *was* helpful.

"He rushes the net too much, so I can win a lot of points with passing shots. If he gets behind quickly, he can get discouraged and lose his concentration. When his first serve is a fault, his second serve can be real weak. And he wears dorky clothes."

His dad had been smiling, but he looked annoyed at Steve's last statement. "How about trying to be serious? All right?"

"Sorry," Steve mumbled.

His dad nodded. "Okay. What are his strengths?"

"Strong first serve, killer backhand, real tough at the net. If I don't hit a passing shot while he's coming in, I have to try to back him off with high lobs or he'll kill me."

Mr. Greeley smiled again. "Good." He looked around. "Where is Charlie, anyway?"

Steve shrugged and picked up a racket. Charlie, he thought with a touch of envy, knew better than to show up any earlier than necessary on a day like this. They weren't due on the court for half an hour, and it wasn't going to help his game at all to sit around like this, whatever his dad thought.

Mr. Greeley moved over next to his son and sighed. "I envy you, Steve. You know why?"

Steve knew exactly what was coming, but also knew better than to say so.

"I envy you because you've got a chance. A real chance. The thing that really gets me," his dad went on, as he had done a hundred times before, "is that I'll *never know*. Maybe I would have been a major star, and maybe not.

"But I would rather have been a complete flop as a pro than never to have had my shot." His father shook his head sadly. "At least that way, I'd be sure that I just didn't have what it takes. It would have been tough at first, but I would have gotten over it, and I would know that I had given it my best and failed."

He laid a hand on Steve's leg. "I don't want you to feel that way when you're my age — wondering what might have been, 'if only.' What worries me about you, Champ, is that you'll blow your opportunity and then wake up when it's too late and start kicking yourself."

"I know, Dad," Steve replied. He couldn't look his father in the eye. His unspoken thought was, *It won't happen to me, because making it as a pro doesn't matter to me the way it did to you, or the way it does to Ginny. But I can't tell you that. I wish I could, but I just can't.*

"How about giving me a hint about your big surprise?" he asked his father. "Is it something that plays CDs?"

Mr. Greeley smiled and shook his head. "It's better that I don't say anything yet. All I can tell you is, you want to look good out there today."

"Hey, Steve, how're you doing?" Charlie Silver, with a smile on his face, walked down to where the Greeleys sat. "Sure is hot out there. Hi, Mr. Greeley."

Mr. Greeley nodded but didn't smile back. Steve saw that his father had his "game face" on, as if *he* were the one who was going out to face Charlie in a little while.

Steve managed to keep a straight face at the sight of Charlie's ugly shirt with big diamond-shaped patches of purple and green. No one who dressed like that could ever be a champion, he decided. Who picks those shirts? Maybe he's color-blind.

"I'm doing great," Steve said, standing up. "Tell you what, I'll make sure we're not out in the hot sun too long, all right?"

Charlie laughed. "You mean you'll let me whip you real fast today? Is that what he means, Mr. Greeley?"

Steve's father scowled. He didn't like to joke about tennis matches.

But Steve grinned. "That wasn't what I had in mind."

A minute later, a man stuck his head into the locker room. "Steve Greeley, Charlie Silver? You guys ready?"

"Right here," said Steve.

"All set," Charlie called out.

"Good, we'll be ready for you in five minutes," the man replied. "I'll come and get you. Stay in here and keep cool as long as you can. It's brutal out there."

Steve snorted. "Tell us something we don't know."

Nobody said anything for the next few minutes. For all that he'd been joking around, Steve thought

10

Charlie looked nervous. He himself was mostly thinking about how hot and uncomfortable he'd been just sitting and watching his sister. Now he'd have to hustle . . . well, a little, anyway.

The tournament official returned to the locker room. "Okay, guys, let's go. Your turn in the steam room."

3

The stands were more than half full when the two players came out on the court, and there was some cheerful applause. Steve blinked in the bright sunshine and looked around. His father yelled something about hanging tough and headed for a seat. Steve heard a few voices call out his name as he put down his spare rackets, a windbreaker (totally unnecessary), and several towels (very necessary). He did a few stretches to limber up.

As hot as it had been in the stands, it was even hotter on the court, he decided. Either the temperature had gone up or the all-weather surface of the court was acting as a giant sun reflector. Whatever the reason, he would have to make sure he drank plenty of liquids today, to make up for all the sweating he'd be doing.

The umpire spun a racket and Steve called, "Up." The racket came down with the logo on the end of it facing up, which meant that Steve would serve first.

He and Charlie began warming up, hitting balls back and forth, using both forehand and backhand, not working too hard at it. Steve felt loose and ready to go in a couple of minutes. He called to Charlie, "You ready?"

Charlie nodded. Both boys turned and signaled the umpire, who was now sitting in his chair at one side of the net, that they were all set to go.

The umpire turned on his microphone. "This is a quarterfinal match in the boys' twelve and under class. The players are Charlie Silver, on my right, and Steve Greeley, on my left. Steve will serve first. The players may begin."

Steve decided to start off by testing Charlie's backhand. He bounced the fuzzy green ball a few times, paused, then tossed the ball high. His racket flashed as it swung around and connected. It was a hard serve into the far corner of the service box, right where he'd wanted it to go.

Bet you don't get a good piece of that, Steve thought as he charged the net.

Sure enough, Charlie's return was soft and right in the middle of the court. Steve drove a hard overhead smash into the opposite corner. Charlie didn't even try to reach it.

"Fifteen–love," said the umpire.

Maybe this will be over fast, Steve thought as he ambled to the other side of the court to serve again. He aimed for the centerline to work on Charlie's backhand again.

This time, however, Charlie was expecting it and hit a nice return that Steve had to hustle to reach. Steve's return hit the top of the net and dropped over, but Charlie had been coming in and hit a high lob toward the baseline. Steve circled around to use his forehand and drove it straight down the line. Charlie lunged but just got the edge of his racket on the ball. The ball bounced harmlessly off the court.

"Thirty–love," said the umpire. Steve's face was flushed and damp with sweat as he prepared to serve again. He spotted his father sitting in the stands, with Ginny next to him. Mr. Greeley pumped his fist in the air in a gesture of encouragement and turned to say something to a man on his other side. Steve didn't recognize the guy, who looked to be somewhat older than his dad, with a deep tan, wearing metallic sunglasses. The stranger nodded at whatever his father had said but looked serious and hard to read behind the shades.

Charlie won that point, but Steve hit a service ace — a serve his opponent couldn't even hit — then walloped a shot that just nicked the baseline to take the first game. The two boys switched sides, as per the rules of play. Switching sides after every odd-numbered game meant neither player was forced to play the entire match at a disadvantage — with the sun in his eyes or on a cracked or uneven surface, for example.

Charlie's first serve sailed long, well out of bounds.

"Fault!" called a linesperson.

Remembering that Charlie's second service was often weak, Steve crept in a few feet, inside the baseline. Sure enough, the serve was soft. Steve hit a wicked cross-court forehand that Charlie couldn't get to.

Love–fifteen.

Then Charlie found his stroke and hit a sizzling service ace that caught Steve by surprise. Charlie methodically began to run Steve back and forth on the baseline, the way Ginny had done with her opponent earlier. Steve lost the game and found that he was beginning to huff and puff a bit.

Both boys held their service for the next four games. Steve decided that he had to pace himself and not run out of energy. At three games apiece, Steve faulted on his first serve, hitting it wide, and then hit one into the net.

"Double fault," the umpire announced. "Love–fifteen."

Steve was angry with himself. His game plan had been to get ahead of Charlie early so that the other boy would lose confidence, then coast to a win. But Charlie wasn't folding; in fact, he was making Steve work for most of his points.

Wiping his face, Steve glanced into the stands. His father was glaring at him. The stranger next to him wore a bland expression. Only Ginny gave a smile of encouragement.

He took a deep breath and tried to focus on what he had to do. From the left side of the baseline, he served down the centerline, hoping to get a weak backhand return. But Charlie saw it coming, shifted around, and hit a dynamite forehand that kicked up chalk in the corner.

Love–thirty.

Steve hit his next serve just beyond the other baseline for a fault, and followed it with a tentative, weak second serve. Charlie pounced on it and hit a winner down the line.

Love–forty. Charlie needed only one more point to take the game.

Steve bent over and rested his hands on his knees. Was it possible that he could lose this match? In this heat, did he really care? Did tennis matter to him all that much?

4

Steve tried to hit an ace on the following serve, but it was long again. Then he doubled-faulted. Charlie had broken his serve and led, four games to three.

Steve knew he had to break Charlie's serve — to win the game even though Charlie was serving — but he didn't know if he had the energy or the will. The two boys walked to the chairs to sit for a moment before changing ends. As Steve slumped in his chair, wiping his face with a towel, he heard Ginny's voice behind him.

"Hey, suck it up, bro. You can beat this guy, and you know it."

Slowly Steve lifted his head and stared at his sister. He didn't say anything, but he knew he must have looked beat.

Ginny stood in front of the stands and leaned forward. "Just remember, he's hot and miserable, too. Look at him."

Steve glanced at Charlie, who sat with his shoulders hunched forward and a towel over his head. His ugly shirt was dripping. When he removed the towel, Charlie's face was flushed and shiny with sweat, and his hair was plastered down. Ginny was right: Charlie looked just like he felt.

He looked up into the stands, where his father was talking to the man in the next seat, pointing in Steve's direction. The man nodded but said nothing, and his expression never changed.

I have to win this, Steve thought. I can't disappoint Dad. He stood up and walked to the baseline, twirling his racket, trying to psych himself up. I can beat Charlie, he told himself. He must feel about as bad as I do. I just have to get the momentum back.

He set himself for Charlie's serve, bouncing lightly on his toes. Charlie smashed the ball, which hit the top of the net . . .

"Let!" called an official.

. . . and bounced back on Charlie's side.

"Fault!" called the umpire.

Steve moved in a few steps, knowing Charlie tended to be cautious with his second serve. He was right. He returned the serve with a hard cross-court shot, racing toward the net as he did so. Charlie's return was weak and Steve hit a volley that Charlie just missed returning.

It was love–fifteen.

Charlie followed his next serve to the net, but Steve hit a high lob that forced him to retreat to the baseline. Both players remained on the baseline, smashing groundstrokes and waiting for the other to make a mistake. Charlie won the point when Steve mis-hit a shot that went wide.

Then Charlie double-faulted, making the score fifteen–thirty. It looked to Steve as if Charlie was tiring fast.

On the next point Steve tested him. He moved him from side to side with well-placed strokes, then rushed the net for a beautiful overhead smash to Charlie's backhand. Charlie couldn't return it and Steve led, fifteen–forty.

When Charlie charged the net on his next serve, Steve hit a perfect shot down the line that Charlie's desperate lunge didn't reach. Game to Greeley. He had broken Charlie and the set was tied, four games apiece.

Over the applause of the crowd, Steve heard his father's shrill, approving whistle. He grinned up at him, and Ginny gave him a big smile.

Steve took the next game without Charlie getting a point and pulled ahead in the match, five–four.

If I win the next one, the set is mine, Steve thought as he waited for Charlie's first serve. Then I just have to win six more games and I can call it a day.

Charlie bounced the ball a few times, then socked a solid serve down the line. He tried to come to the net, but Steve forced him back with a lob and kept him there by smashing his next two returns to the baseline.

When Charlie stumbled after the second return, Steve hit a soft drop shot that barely cleared the net. Charlie rushed forward but couldn't reach the ball. The score was love–fifteen.

Charlie took a lot of time before his next serve, trying to get his breath and his energy back. But his first serve went into the net for a fault, and Steve put the easy second serve away with a cross-court backhand into the corner. Steve thought Charlie looked beat, mentally and physically.

But he was wrong. Charlie surprised Steve with a sliced serve that spun away from him into the corner for an ace. He wasn't finished yet, obviously.

The score was fifteen–thirty. Steve wanted to finish the set quickly, ideally by breaking Charlie again, right now.

Charlie hit a serve straight at Steve, apparently hoping that Steve wouldn't react fast enough to return effectively. Steve jumped to his left and hit a forehand that nicked the top of the net. Charlie was caught leaning in the wrong direction and couldn't get to it.

Fifteen–forty. Steve now had three chances to take the set point, the point that would win him the first set. Then Charlie hit a topspin serve that took an extralong bounce. Steve mis-hit it, bringing the score to thirty–forty. But Steve still had one more chance to score the winning point.

This time, when Charlie tried the same kind of serve, it landed outside the service box for a fault. On the second serve, Charlie played it cautious.

Steve smashed a return that forced Charlie back

behind the baseline. Charlie returned it right where Steve had hoped he would. It was in a perfect position for him to put it away in the opposite corner, far out of Charlie's reach.

"Game and set, Greeley," the umpire called. "He leads one set to none."

The players could now go to the air-conditioned locker room, towel off, put on dry shirts, and take a short rest. Sitting down and taking deep breaths, Steve decided that he was in control now. Charlie had seemed to fold under pressure in their past matches, and he would again. Steve wouldn't have to work as hard in the next set. He hoped.

5

Hey, Champ!" Steve looked up to find his father peeking in at him around the locker room door. Mr. Greeley came over and punched his son lightly on the arm. "You had me worried there for a minute," he said quietly. He squatted down facing Steve and kept his voice to a whisper so Charlie wouldn't overhear him.

"Now let's see you kick it into overdrive for the second set. You have him on the ropes. Don't let him get back into the match. I know you can do it." He stood up and looked down at his son. "Right?"

Steve smiled and nodded. Kick it into overdrive, he thought. It's easy for *you* to say, you're not out there broiling on the court.

"I'll do my best," he assured his father, who smiled and left the room.

An official came in to get the boys. "Okay, guys," he said, "time to go. You two feel all right? No problems with the heat?"

Steve and Charlie exchanged a glance and a tired smile.

"*What* heat?" asked Charlie.

"Never felt better," said Steve.

The official chuckled. "That's the spirit."

Back on the court, Steve could swear that it had gotten even hotter. The people in the bleachers were waving their programs like fans. They were too hot to applaud the players as they reached the court, except for Ginny and Mr. Greeley, who clapped and whistled. Only the mysterious stranger beside his father looked cool and calm behind his mirrored shades.

Since Charlie had served the previous game, Steve served to open the second set. Wanting to conserve his energy, he stayed behind the baseline instead of charging the net. Charlie was content to stay back, too. The game went on and on as the boys stroked the ball back and forth. Finally, Steve won the game when Charlie's attempted passing shot went wide.

Charlie won the second game, although Steve thought he might have been able to, if he had been willing to chase every ball and fight hard for every point — which he wasn't.

Charlie must have gotten a second wind, fueled by winning that game, because he suddenly began to play more energetically, coming to the net to volley and racing after Steve's attempts at passing shots. He broke Steve's serve to go ahead two games to one.

Sitting and toweling off before switching to the other end of the court, Steve concentrated on psyching himself up and finding the energy he needed to come back and win the match. He didn't look forward to facing his father if he lost. That, more than the possibility of losing, was what he wanted to avoid. Even having to go three sets to win would upset his dad. Got to win this set somehow, he told himself. *Got* to.

Charlie seemed to be feeling the heat again and started missing first serves. Steve took two quick points by coming in on the soft second serves and slamming passing shots out of Charlie's reach. A double fault by Charlie made it love–forty.

Charlie finally got a first serve into the box and charged the net. Steve forced him back with a lob and raced after Charlie's overhand smash, making the return with a desperate dive. Charlie netted his forehand return, and Steve had broken back to tie the set at two games apiece.

That shot was the turning point. Steve held his own serve, bringing the score to three games to two. Then Charlie lost his cool, even losing a point on a foot fault. Steve took that game to go up by four games to two. Three games later, he'd won the set six–three to take the match.

He took a deep breath and went to the net to shake hands with his opponent, and the two boys walked off, hot and tired. The remaining crowd seemed to be more interested in finding some shade than in applauding, except for Ginny.

Mr. Greeley came down to meet Steve as he was toweling himself off. Steve looked up, hoping to get congratulations on the win, but his father just frowned.

"You have to work on that killer instinct, son. You almost let him off the hook there. I don't think you showed a lot of 'want-to' today. Also, you should have anticipated some of his moves, especially in the second set. I have some notes for you, some stuff we have to work on, but we can save that for tonight, after dinner. Right now, there's someone I want you to meet. Come on."

As his dad turned and walked away, Steve stared after him for a moment.

Even when I win, he thought, I can't win.

6

Ginny ran up to her brother as he slowly walked toward the locker room. "All *right!*" she yelled, giving him a whack on the arm. "Way to go!"

Steve sighed. "Thanks, but I wish Dad felt that way. He says I don't have the 'killer instinct.'"

Ginny shook her head and turned to look at their father as he joined the mysterious stranger in the stands. "He doesn't make it easy on you."

"Hey, I didn't congratulate *you*," Steve said. "You looked tough out there today. What was the final score?"

"Six–two, six–zero," Ginny replied, trying to sound casual but looking delighted by the result.

Steve whistled. "All right, Gin! Awesome! Uh, sorry we didn't stay till the end, but . . ."

Ginny held up her hands. "Don't tell me, I know. You had to take an hour 'getting ready' for your match." Her face took on a wistful look. "I wish Dad would give me that kind of attention."

She brightened. "You know who the guy is with Dad, by the way?"

"He didn't say. Who is he?"

Ginny smiled. "I'll let Dad tell you. He's the surprise he was telling you about before."

Steve's face fell. "*He's* the surprise? I was hoping for a CD player."

Ginny laughed. "This is better than a CD player any day. Go on, they're waiting for you in the locker room."

Steve felt too hot, tired, and discouraged to take any satisfaction in knowing that he had beaten Charlie Silver and would advance to the semifinals. Then, on his way to the locker room, he saw someone who made his mood lighten. It was his buddy Pat Carbo.

"Hey, awesome match!" Pat yelled. After Ginny, Pat was Steve's biggest supporter.

Pat and Steve had learned the game of tennis together, when they were eight years old. Steve's father had taught them himself, setting up a rigorous schedule of practices. Pat had stuck with it for a summer but then bowed out when he realized he liked soccer much better.

The rigorous practices had continued for Steve, however. He'd been a little lonely at first, but then Ginny had started playing, too. Mr. Greeley had been reluctant for her to join in, but Mrs. Greeley had insisted.

So now, three times a week for two hours at a time, Mr. Greeley worked with his children on forehands, backhands, volleys, serves, and lobs. He coached them on ways to draw opponents out of position. He taught them where to aim the ball to bounce to make it impossible for an opponent to return. He showed them the tricks a ball could do with just a bit of spin applied by the racket.

Steve couldn't imagine his life without tennis, but sometimes he wished his father didn't work him so hard. Still, hard work paid off — he'd just won the quarterfinals, hadn't he?

"Thanks, Pat," Steve said now, smiling. "Listen, my dad's waiting to talk to me. I'll catch up to you later, okay? Maybe we can go for ice cream or something."

"You got it, Ace," Pat said, shooting a finger at him.

Steve walked into the locker room, where his father stood with the stranger from the stands. Mr. Greeley was talking earnestly to this man, who, Steve noted, still wore his mirrored shades.

"Here he is now," his father said, turning and gesturing to his son.

He looks nervous, Steve thought. Who is this guy?

"Vince, this is my boy, Steve. Steve, I want you to meet Vince Marino. *The* Vince Marino."

Steve knew the name and suddenly understood why his dad was so excited. Vince Marino ran a famous tennis school and camp in Florida. He had developed some of the top pros in the game. His dad had shown him a magazine article about Vince, with pictures of some of Vince's past students. A few had won major titles: the U.S. Open, Wimbledon, the French Open, and so on.

Vince took off his sunglasses, smiled, and stuck out his hand. When Steve shook it, he found that the hand was strong and callused. Coming from Florida as he did perhaps explained why he hadn't been sweating in this heat.

"Congratulations, Steve," Mr. Marino said. His voice was low-pitched, and he seemed to radiate energy. "I was impressed with the way you bore down when the crunch was on."

"Thanks," Steve muttered, feeling self-conscious. This guy had trained some greats.

"I can see that you inherited your dad's talent," Mr. Marino continued. "Did your dad tell you we went to college together? Ted was our number one player, and I was number four. You should have seen him back then. He really had the goods."

Steve's father jumped in quickly. "You know about Vince's training center, Steve. If someone does well working with Vince, it's practically a ticket to the pro tour — Vince makes careers."

"Sure," Steve said. "I read about you, Mr. Marino. It sounds pretty awesome, your camp."

Mr. Marino smiled again. "Your father has been bending my ear about you for years now, but I hadn't been able to come see you compete until now. Looks to me like you have a lot of potential."

"Even if you gave Charlie more of a chance than you should have," Mr. Greeley added hastily. "I figured you'd romp today, son. What happened?"

What happened? Steve thought. What happened was, I won in straight sets even though it was a hundred degrees out there. But that's not good enough for you, is it?

"Well, we'll work on a few things later," his father went on. "I've been telling Vince that you'd be a great candidate for his summer training program. What would you think about going down to Florida this summer?"

"Whoa," Mr. Marino said, holding up his hand as if he were directing traffic. "Let's not rush things. It's not a done deal yet, Steve. I'm going to watch your semifinal tomorrow, and I also need to talk to you and your parents for a while before anything is definite. But I will say this: I have a couple of openings, and you're certainly in the running — probably a front runner."

Steve blinked. Go to Florida and play tennis all summer? Did he really want that? "Uh . . . thanks, Mr. Marino, that sounds . . ."

"Call me Vince from now on," said the coach, patting Steve on the shoulder. "After the buildup Ted has given me, I feel like I've known you for years.

The thing you need to consider, very carefully, is this: Do you *want* to commit yourself to my camp?"

Steve's father stared at his old friend in disbelief. "Does he *want* to? Are you kidding? Why should that even come up? It's the chance of a lifetime! Of *course* he wants to!"

But Vince was now focusing on Steve. "You enjoy tennis, Steve, I know that. But how important is it to you? Is it just a game you're good at and have fun with? Or is it something you want to excel at, no matter what? That's what I want you to think about for the next few days."

He looked Steve in the eye.

"Because if you don't care enough about tennis to live, eat, drink, and dream about it for a long time, maybe my place isn't for you. You're a nice young man, and your dad and I go way back. But you'd better be ready to work your tail off if you come down to Florida."

Vince counted off on his fingers. "At the summer camp, you'll be expected to work at least six hours a day, six days a week. You'll work at building up your stamina and strength. You'll practice every part of the game — service, return of service, volleying, ground strokes, half-volley, the works — until you can do it all in your sleep. This is not your fun-and-games summer camp; it's more like boot camp for tennis rookies. See what I mean?"

"He can do whatever you ask of him," Mr. Greeley insisted. "Don't you worry about that. I know my son."

But Steve had listened to Vince describe the program with mounting anxiety. Now that school was out, he'd been looking forward to kicking back and having fun with Pat and his other friends: going to the beach, catching all the cool summer movies, hanging out at the mall with his buddies . . . and playing some tennis, too, but just for fun. Doing nothing but working on tennis sounded more like going to school, but without any variety. How much did tennis matter to him?

Not as much as it mattered to his dad, for sure. His dad would feel awful if Steve simply turned down this chance. And maybe he didn't want to turn it down. Maybe the camp would turn out to be fantastic. *Ginny* would think it was fantastic. Right now, he didn't know how to answer Vince.

There was a long silence, during which his father stared at him, looking upset.

Finally, Steve managed to stammer a reply. "That's . . . it sounds really . . . amazing, Mr. — Vince. I guess I'll think about it real hard."

Vince nodded. "Good. You do that. I think you have the physical skills and talent to be a fine tennis player. But it takes more than that. You have to *want* it, bad. And you're really the only one who knows for sure if you do."

Steve and his father joined Vince as he headed outside. As Vince came through the door, he almost ran over Ginny, who was waiting just outside.

Ginny looked awed, as if she had just run into her favorite movie or rock star. "Mr. Marino? My dad didn't really get a chance to introduce us before. I'm Ginny. It's an honor to meet you. I've read all about your school. I'd love to play pro tennis in a few years, and your school would be perfect for —"

"Ginny," Mr. Greeley interrupted with a warning in his voice.

But Vince smiled at Ginny. "You were in the quarters today, right?"

"Yeah!" Ginny nodded, her face lit up by a proud

smile. "I won six–two, six–zero. I'll have a semi to-morrow, a little before Steve."

"I wasn't aware of that." Vince looked from Ginny to her father and back. "Well, I'll definitely come and watch you."

Ginny's eyes grew wide. "*Would* you, Mr. Marino?"

"Call me Vince," said the coach.

"That'd be awesome, knowing you're in the stands, Mr. — Vince."

"Sure thing," Vince said, and turned to Mr. Gree-ley. "I have to go make some calls. Walk me to my car, okay?"

Steve watched them leave. His father was talk-ing eagerly, probably trying to persuade Vince that Steve really, truly wanted to spend his summer liv-ing and breathing tennis. But Steve felt sure that Vince had his doubts.

Just like he did.

Ginny poked her brother in the ribs. "So? What'd he have to say? Are you going to his camp?"

Steve shrugged. "I don't know. I don't even know if I *want* to go. Dad —"

"Don't know if you want to . . ." Ginny was aston-ished. "*Why?* How can you pass this up?"

"You know what they do at that camp?" Steve demanded. "They play tennis. All the time. Every day. Nothing but tennis. I mean, they let you eat and sleep, I guess, but otherwise, it's just tennis."

Ginny sighed. "Yeah, isn't it wonderful?"

"No, it's not!" exclaimed Steve. "I mean, I know you think it's wonderful, but I might hate it! Dad thinks it's wonderful, too, and when he saw I wasn't all that happy with the idea, he looked as if I had just forgotten his birthday. I don't know what I'm going to do."

Ginny shook her head. "Yeah, I see what you mean. I guess I was only thinking about how great it'd be for me to go there. Working on my game all summer sounds like heaven. But you're not into tennis like I am."

"Not yet, anyway. Maybe I might feel different about it in a few years, but right now, there're too many other things I enjoy, too much I'd miss if I went to that camp. But how can I tell Dad?"

Ginny shrugged. "Tell you what, I'll think about how you can break the news to Dad, and you think about how you can get him to think about my tennis career the way he thinks about yours. Is that a deal?"

Steve grinned and stuck out a hand, which Ginny shook. "At least we can level with each other," he said.

Ginny laughed. "You're lucky that you'll never have to play me. I'd level you in a whole different way."

"I'll bet you would, too," replied Steve, giving Ginny an admiring look.

7

That night before dinner, Ginny and Steve sat quietly as their father told Steve what had been wrong with his play that afternoon.

"I can tell from your body language, the way you stand, when you're giving it a hundred percent. Half the time today, you weren't. If you'd been totally involved, Charlie would've been lucky to win more than a couple of games."

"It was hot out there," muttered Steve.

"I know it was hot. But if you'd played hard the whole time, the match would have been over that much more quickly. Also, we're going to have to work on your passing shots. If they'd been sharper, Charlie wouldn't have been able to rush the net so often. Maybe we can get in some practice time tomorrow on that. And your topspin serve."

"What was wrong with my topspin serve?" Steve asked. "It was working well, I thought."

"It could be better, Champ. It should really leap off the court. Yours needs a bit more juice on it."

"Dad?" Ginny said. "What about my match? Got any notes for me?"

Mr. Greeley looked startled. "Notes for you, honey? Hey, you won six–two, six–zero. What else is there to say?"

Ginny wouldn't give up. "Well, is there anything you think I should work on? Anything you might want to help me with?"

He shook his head. "Not really, Gin. I mean, I didn't see the whole match, but from what I saw, you're doing all the right things."

Although it sounded like a compliment, Steve saw that Ginny didn't look too happy.

Mrs. Greeley came in from the kitchen with dinner. Steve hoped that the conversation could now take a new turn. But no such luck.

"It's just too bad that you had to have an off day when Vince was there," Mr. Greeley said as he helped himself to some lasagna. "Maybe I should have warned you that he was coming."

"He seemed to think I did pretty well," answered Steve.

"Oh, sure, sure." He patted his son's shoulder. "But impressing that guy is really important. It's amazing what Vince can do for a young athlete."

He laid his fork down and gripped Steve's arm. "When I was your age, there was nothing like Vince's school around, anywhere. I mean, sure, there were coaches, and there were schools and camps you could go to, but Vince has taken it to a new level. He has all these specialists working with him, people who give you advice on what to eat, what exercises help you, the best shoes and rackets, you name it. And then the fact that people will know you worked with Vince — that matters, too. This'll give you a major boost."

He let go of Steve's arm and picked up his fork again.

"Good thing that Vince and I are buddies from way back," he continued, punctuating his remark with a forkful of pasta, "or you might not have been selected. Good as you are, Champ, you'd just be one of a hundred gifted kids, all hoping for a shot. Now, you're almost sure to make it, thanks to me."

Steve sneaked a look at Ginny, who rolled her eyes at him. Steve just barely managed to keep himself from laughing.

"And, Champ, always keep this in mind: You *are* good. Take it from me, you have the total package. Your serve is lethal, and you can place it wherever you want. You've got better coordination than any boy your age I've seen. Your foot speed is great, too. If you could just learn to concentrate a little more, get your head completely into the game, there'd be no stopping you. I really think you have more going for you than I did when I was young. Can you imagine being at the top of the heap? Playing all over the world, meeting the best, becoming a star?"

"That's . . . pretty exciting, Dad," Steve said, toying with his mostly uneaten food. "I just get worried sometimes. I hope I don't disappoint you, that's all."

"How could you disappoint me?" His dad leaned forward. "Just knowing that you're giving it a hundred and ten percent out there, that's good enough for me. And it'll be good enough to succeed, too. I'm sure of it."

"Dad," said Ginny, "is there any chance that Vince could find room for *me* at his camp? I'd do anything

44

to work with him. It'd be great to spend the summer there. Could you ask him for me? Please?"

Mr. Greeley blinked in surprise and seemed stuck for a reply. But Mrs. Greeley, who had been silent this whole time, jumped in first.

"Honey, I thought we talked about this. You need to go to summer school this year and work on your math. It's your weakest subject, and it's so important these days."

Ginny sighed. "Mom, I want to be a pro tennis player. And I think I can do it, too. I'm going to be the state champ of the fourteen-and-unders. No one is going to beat me this year."

Mrs. Greeley's tone got firmer. "Ginny, tennis can wait. We agreed about this."

"Yeah, but we had that talk before Vince showed up." Ginny looked from one parent to the other. "Don't you see? This changes things. If I could be coached by Vince Marino, I might be ready for the pros real soon. School wouldn't matter. *Math* wouldn't matter. That's what I want, more than anything else in the world. Mom? Dad?"

"What *I* see," Mrs. Greeley answered, "is that you aren't thinking straight about your future yet. You're absolutely sure you'll be successful as a tennis player. But what if you're not?"

Ginny opened her mouth to protest, but Mrs. Greeley went on. "I'm not doubting your talent, sweetie. Or your determination — we all know you've got plenty of that. But there are a lot of talented young athletes out there who all want the same thing, and all of them are sure they'll be the one to do it — and most of them are wrong. Also, even if you're the best tennis player ever, you might get hurt and end your career that way. Look at what happened to your father. Luckily, he was smart enough to stay in school."

Mrs. Greeley took hold of one of Ginny's hands.

"If you don't succeed in tennis, and you've neglected your education, what will you do then? The world is a very tough place for a young person without proper schooling."

Ginny removed her hand, her face sullen. "I can always go back to school afterward. I may never get another chance to go to Vince's camp. This happens once in a lifetime."

Mr. Greeley cleared his throat. "I think your mom

is right about this, sweetie. You need to stay in school, and you need to get your math up to speed."

Ginny's jaw was clenched. "Oh, sure. *I* have to worry about school, but *Steve* doesn't have to. *He* can go to Florida if he wants. Thanks a lot."

Steve felt awful, but he didn't know what to say. So he said nothing.

Dinner finished in gloomy silence.

8

After dinner, Steve found Ginny sitting alone in the dark in the backyard, staring up at the night sky. He sat down next to her.

"Hi. Okay if I sit here?"

"It's your house, too," she muttered.

"Lighten up," he said. "You know how I feel. I was hoping to spend the summer having some fun around here instead of playing tennis thirty hours a day. And I know you'd love to go to Florida and come back ready for the pros."

"But *noo-o-o-o*," Ginny snarled. "I have to work on my *math*. Like *math* is really going to help me sharpen my game. The only math I care about is fifteen, thirty, forty, game."

"Well," — Steve sprawled on his back in the grass

next to his sister — "Mom's just worried about what'd happen if you don't make it to the pros."

"I can't think about that now," Ginny said. "I have to think positive about tennis. You understand, don't you?"

"Sure," said Steve quickly.

"Well, you're the only one in this family who does, then. Mom doesn't think I can make it, and Dad is too wrapped up in your game to have any time for mine."

Steve sighed. "You're not the only one with problems. You think I'm happy being the one Dad is always pushing? You think it's easy?"

Ginny reached over to pat her brother's arm. "No, I know it's not easy. But sooner or later, you know you're going to have to tell him the truth. The longer you wait, the harder it'll be."

"I know," admitted Steve. "But I don't know how to do it. He's going to be so unhappy." He sighed. "I just can't, not yet. It'll be as if I insulted him or something."

Ginny sat up. "You don't have to say you don't want to play tennis, period. Just say you're still not sure you want to be a pro. That way, he can still hope you'll come around to see things his way. And who knows, maybe you will, someday."

Steve brightened. "Yeah, you're right. If I just say I need more time, he probably wouldn't be totally disappointed. That's what I should do."

"Hey, if you tell him that, maybe Dad will pay more attention to *me*," Ginny said. "Maybe he'll go to work to persuade Mom and Vince that I should go to tennis camp this summer and work on math another time." She grabbed Steve's hand. "*Would* you? Will you talk to Dad and maybe put in a good word for me while you're doing it?"

Steve hesitated. "I . . . yeah, I'll talk to him. I'll tell him that I'm not ready yet, that I need a little more time before I can —"

"Hey, Champ, Gin, it's getting late." Their father stood behind them by the back door. Steve wondered how much of the conversation he had overheard.

But if Mr. Greeley had heard anything, he gave no sign of it. "You both have important matches tomorrow and you need your rest. How about turning in?"

"Sure, Dad," Ginny said as she scrambled to her

feet. "By the way, Dad, there's something Steve needs to talk to you about. Right, Steve?"

"What's on your mind, Champ?" asked their father.

Steve suddenly felt tongue-tied. He couldn't think of a word to say. "Uh . . . nothing, Dad. It'll keep."

"*Steve!*" whispered Ginny, with a pleading expression on her face.

"Not now," Steve replied. "I feel really tired, and I better get to sleep."

He hurried inside, not wanting to face Ginny. He knew she was mad, and he felt guilty, as though he had betrayed her. But if he was going to tell his father the truth, he wanted to do it his own way.

He *would.* He had to. And soon.

When Steve poked his head out the window the following morning, he was relieved to find that the weather had cooled down. It was a great day for tennis, and he was actually looking forward to the semifinal match.

His mood dampened a little at breakfast. Ginny wouldn't look at him, and he knew that she was angry with him for not speaking up to their father the night before.

"Gin?" he said. She stared straight ahead as if he hadn't spoken. "Listen, I'm really sorry about last night, but, hey, I *know* I said I'd tell Dad I wasn't sure about a tennis career, but it . . . didn't seem like the right time."

"The *right time?*" She sneered at him as she

echoed his words. "Face it, bro, you just chickened out. I think there's never going to be a right time."

"That's not so!" Steve's face felt hot, and he knew it was beet-red, which happened when he got mad or embarrassed. "I *am* going to tell him, and real soon. I just . . . need a little time to figure out what to say. But I'll do it."

"Uh-huh. Well, I'll believe it when I see it," Ginny said, slamming her juice glass down in front of her.

"Morning, all," said Mr. Greeley, smiling as he sat down at the table. Steve and Ginny muttered their greetings. Their father gave no sign of being aware of the tension in the air.

"Looks like a perfect day for tennis," he said. "Is everybody ready to go?"

Both his children nodded, and he seemed satisfied.

"Great, great. Ginny, who are you playing in the semis?"

"Maddy Stern. She can be a little troublesome," she said. "I was thinking I'd use my topspin serve on her right from the start. What do you think?"

"Hmm, I don't think I know your opponent. But

I'm sure you know the best way to beat her." He gave Ginny a smile, then turned to Steve. "You'll be playing Darren Poole. He's going to be a challenge, a lot more trouble than Charlie Silver was yesterday. You'd better be ready."

Steve chewed on a slice of toast, trying not to see Ginny's unhappy look at the way their father had brushed her aside. "I'll be ready. It's a nicer day, and I got my rest."

"Darren is almost six feet tall, with those long arms, and he has a cannon serve, remember."

"Sure, I remember," Steve said.

Mr. Greeley buttered toast. "How do you deal with that big serve?"

"I back off the baseline. I try to meet the ball and not kill it." Steve drummed his fingers on the table, wishing they could leave so he wouldn't have to see Ginny glaring at him.

"You can win, Champ." He gave his son a tap on the shoulder. "But you'll have to play better than yesterday. Remember, Vince will be watching and you need to look good."

Ginny leaned forward toward her father. "Will Vince watch my match, too?"

Mr. Greeley looked surprised. "I don't know, hon. He said he would, but he might have other players to check out."

"But you could get him to watch Ginny, couldn't you, Dad?" asked Steve.

Mr. Greeley frowned. "I thought we agreed that Ginny will go to summer school this year."

"*I* didn't agree to anything," Ginny snapped. "You and Mom —"

Steve cut her off. "Even if Ginny goes to summer school this year, Vince should look at her, Dad. There'll always be next summer. Ginny wants to work with Vince. Why not have Vince see what she can do, so he'll keep her in mind for next year?"

His father chewed his toast thoughtfully. "Okay. I'm not making any promises, but —"

Ginny flashed Steve a grateful smile. "Thanks, Dad! That'll be great!"

Steve was happy to see that everything was all right between him and Ginny. Now he could concentrate on his game.

Half an hour later, he was trying to do just that. He agreed with his dad about one thing. It was a perfect day for tennis: mild and sunny, with a slight breeze. As he took the court with Darren Poole, Steve went over his plan for beating the other boy.

Darren was a tough competitor who never gave up. He was four inches taller and his long arms gave him a greater reach and a whiplike serve. When he came to the net, his reach made it hard to get a passing shot by him.

Steve had faster reflexes, though, and Darren could be forced into errors if he was run around a lot. But Darren had won two out of their three previous matches. Steve knew he had to win, not just to even that score, but to advance to the finals.

Darren had won the racquet spin to serve first. Just as the game began, Steve glanced at the stands. He spotted his father, mother, and sister sitting halfway up in the stands. Vince sat with them, wearing his mirrored sunglasses. Off to one side sat Pat Carbo.

Darren took the first game easily. His sizzling serves caught the corners and Steve couldn't return them solidly.

On his own first serve Steve charged the net but mis-hit a volley, sending the ball out of bounds and giving Darren a love–fifteen lead.

His next serve was an ace — a beautiful topspin that Darren sprawled after but couldn't get his racket on. Steve stayed on the baseline for the rest of the game, forcing the taller boy into errors with a relentless ground game. Darren was puffing a little after Steve's game point.

Steve glanced up into the stands again. His father was grinning broadly and talking eagerly to Vince, who nodded. Ginny and his mom clapped and gave him the thumbs-up sign.

Both players held serve for the next six games. Steve had one chance to break Darren, but he messed up a volley, hitting what should have been a winner past the baseline.

With the first set at four games apiece, Darren hit a few poor first serves. On one, Steve made a perfect return to Darren's backhand. He put away Darren's weak return shot to make the score love–fifteen. When Darren came to the net on the next point, Steve crossed him up with a shot to his forehand side that Darren couldn't get to.

Each boy won a point, bringing the score to fifteen–forty. Darren sent the ball whizzing down the centerline, but Steve got to it in time. Darren flogged it back to Steve and charged the net. But Steve drove him way back with a lob, then came in himself. Darren stayed behind the baseline, expecting a smash volley, but Steve hit a soft drop shot to win the game.

If Steve held serve, he'd win the first set. Darren knew it, too. He bore down hard on every point, taking no chances, racing for each shot. Steve matched him in intensity, and the game went to forty-all. The crowd was roaring encouragement, obviously enjoying the battle.

Steve's next serve was down the middle, and Darren, caught leaning the wrong way, made his first error of the game. The ball hit the top of the net and dropped back on his side, making it Steve's advantage.

Steve bounced the ball and took a deep breath. He aimed his serve right at Darren and sent the ball over the net with as much force as he could muster. For a split second Darren froze, then managed a tentative return. Steve put it away with an overhead smash.

"Game and set to Greeley," announced the umpire. "He leads one set to none."

Darren looked grim as the second set began. Steve knew that the match was far from over.

The second set was as even as the first had been, but Steve made two more unforced errors on volleys that gave games to Darren. Darren won six games to three, tying the match at one set each. The third set would decide it.

Darren now seemed to get cautious, as if he was more concerned with not losing than with winning. He took a little power off his first serves. When he returned serve, he stopped charging the net and stayed on the baseline.

Steve, on the other hand, played more aggressively. He took advantage of the softer serves to come to the net more often, which got him some points and cost him others. He wished his serve-and-volley game were more consistent. If it had been, he believed he might have taken the third set — and the match — pretty quickly.

As it was, he was leading three games to two after five games, with Darren about to serve. Steve was just behind the baseline, expecting another less-than-sizzling first service. Instead, the ball rocketed into the service box and by him as if it had been shot from a cannon. Before he knew it, Darren had won the game, with two aces and two beautiful volleys.

Now it was Steve who was feeling uncertain. He began the next game with a double fault. He suddenly felt weak, as if he were playing on quicksand with a twenty-pound racket. Darren took the game, with Steve getting just one point. Steve now trailed, three games to four.

Somehow, he knew, he had to get himself together fast. Otherwise he'd lose the match. Even if he didn't care about impressing Vince, he didn't want to lose.

Fortunately, it was time to switch ends of the court, so he had a moment to sit down. He drank something he couldn't even taste and took some deep breaths, leaned back, and shut his eyes for a second. When he opened them, Ginny was watching him from in front of the stands.

"Hey, bro," she called. "Don't panic. Just play your game and you'll beat this guy. He'll run out of gas, you wait and see."

Steve smiled and nodded. He wiped the sweat off his face and stood up.

This time he positioned himself well back of the baseline, and when Darren's rocket serve came, he was ready for it. He returned it with a topspin forehand that darted away from the end of Darren's racket. But on the next point, Darren came back with a sizzling serve right at Steve's chest. Steve couldn't handle it, and the score was even.

Both players sensed that this game was crucial and played as hard as they could. They went to deuce, a tie of forty–forty, and both Steve and Darren survived several game points. Finally, Darren missed a first serve.

Steve decided to gamble. When Darren reared back to serve, Steve moved in front of the baseline.

Sure enough, Darren's second serve was soft. Steve hit an overhead smash, racing to the net behind it. Darren barely got a lob back over the net. Steve put it away with another smash. Advantage, Greeley.

The next point seemed to go on forever. Steve made one incredible diving save, but Darren dashed across the court and returned it. Finally, Darren made an unforced error, hitting what should have been an easy backhand into the net, and the game was Steve's. The set was even at four games apiece.

Both boys held serve for the next four games, making the score six to six and setting up a tie-breaker. Once again they sat down for a few minutes before changing ends of the court.

As he took the court to receive Darren's serve, Steve tried not to think about the ache in his shoulders and back. It had been a long, hard-fought match so far, and now it felt to him like the *real* match was just starting. He hoped that his opponent was feeling some aches and pains, too.

In a tiebreaker, one player serves once, then they take turns serving twice, switching ends after each has served. Whoever gets to seven points first, winning by two, wins.

Darren's first serve didn't give the impression of fatigue. It was another boomer, down the middle, good for an ace. It was Steve's turn to serve, and he hit a solid shot to Darren's backhand side, charging the net as he did. Darren's return was cross-court to his own backhand. Steve lunged for the ball but could only tip it into the net. Darren led two–love.

Steve won the next point after a long baseline-to-baseline duel. But Darren won the next two points on his own serves to lead, four–one.

Steve tried serving straight at Darren's chest, but Darren sidestepped and hit a strong forehand return that Steve had to reach for. His shot tipped the net . . . and bounced softly over for a lucky point.

He took the next point with a beautiful ace, a shot that kicked up chalk in the very corner of the court. The score was now four–three.

The bleachers were completely full, and everyone was standing, cheering and applauding after every point. Steve noticed that even Vince was on his feet.

Darren's next two serves were split and the score was five–four. A single mistake, Steve told himself, would probably cost the match.

He decided to stay aggressive and charged the net behind his serve. But he misjudged Darren's return and the ball swerved into him, caroming off the frame of the racket and plopping into the net. Darren now led six–four. Steve had to win the next two points just to get even. If he lost one, the match was Darren's.

He hit a topspin serve that Darren returned to his forehand. Steve replied with a cross-court smash. Darren dove for it, reached it in the nick of time, but then couldn't recover.

Seeing his opponent off balance at the edge of the court, Steve put away a winner to Darren's backhand side. Six to five, and Steve had to win the next point, too.

He returned Darren's serve deep to Darren's forehand side, and the players began a long baseline exchange, moving each other from side to side. Neither wanted to risk moving in. Steve was tired and hoped Darren was fading too.

Then Darren made a mistake. He started across the baseline before Steve hit the ball, assuming that Steve would want to make him run. But Steve surprised him, hitting the ball down the line to where Darren had just been standing. Darren couldn't backtrack in time. The tiebreaker was knotted at six–six.

Steve was relieved to have a chance to sit down for a moment before they switched ends of the court.

What will Darren do now? he asked himself. He thought back over the match, trying to recall the points Darren had won decisively. His cannon serve had proven to be his best weapon, Steve decided, standing up to return to position on the court.

Darren prepared to serve. With the match on the line, Steve stepped back two paces to get ready for it.

Whap! And here it came, like a blur! Without

thinking — he had no time to think — Steve got his racket behind the ball and sent it back over the net. He moved forward, backhanded the next return across the court, and, when Darren hit a soft, weak lob back, smashed the ball past him. He was at match point and the serve was his.

The crowd was yelling, but Steve barely heard them. He held the ball loosely in his left hand and glanced at Darren. Darren was bouncing on his toes. With a deep breath, Steve tossed the ball up and smashed a topspin serve that tagged the center-line.

Darren lunged after it but couldn't reach it. He lost his footing and fell, then lay motionless for a moment before slowly getting up and walking to the net. Steve shook his hand and trudged toward the sidelines, too tired to celebrate his victory.

11

The first person to reach Steve was Ginny, who threw her arms around him and hugged him happily. Pat Carbo stuck out his hand for a high five. Some adults he didn't know slapped him on the back and congratulated him. Then his father, mother, and Vince appeared. Vince was smiling broadly.

"You looked good out there!" he said. "I'll talk to you later." He turned to Ginny. "I have some phone calls to make, but I'll be back in time to watch your match." He hurried away.

Ginny's smile could have lit up a city.

Pat leaned toward Steve. "Hey, you want to go celebrate at the mall? I'll treat you to a game of pinball."

Steve smiled happily. "Absolutely! I want to watch Gin's match and then let's go."

Mr. Greeley put his arm around Steve's shoulders. "You made me proud out there, son. You really did."

Steve was startled and pleased by the praise. "Thanks, Dad."

His father nodded and continued. "I just have a few notes for you . . . there are some things we have to work on before the finals. Especially your serve-and-volley game. That hurt you today."

At first Steve wasn't sure he was hearing right. Was his father *criticizing* the match he'd just played? He realized he had heard correctly and his body sagged.

Mrs. Greeley had heard, too, and said, *"Ted,"* in a warning voice.

"What?" demanded their father, looking bewildered. "I *said* he did a good job! I just wanted to point out a couple of problems, while they were fresh in my mind, that's all."

"You can talk about that later," his mother said, frowning at him. "Let Steve enjoy his victory for a little while, all right?"

"I'm happy he won!" Mr. Greeley looked confused, as though he couldn't understand what the problem was. "I just wanted —"

"Dad, can we talk about my mistakes later?" asked Steve. *"Please?"*

His father shrugged. "Okay, okay. Just as long as we do it. How about after Ginny's match?"

Steve nodded. "For a few minutes, all right."

Ginny glanced at her watch. "Speaking of my match, I have to get going. Bye, guys."

"Good luck, hon," called Mrs. Greeley as Ginny hurried away.

"Go get her!" yelled Steve.

Ginny waved in response as she headed toward the locker room.

"Who's she playing?" his father asked.

Steve was startled that his father had forgotten their breakfast conversation. "She's playing Maddy Stern. Ginny should romp."

"I'm sure she will," his father said, as they made their way to the court where Ginny's game would be played.

Just before Ginny served to begin the match, Vince ran up and joined the Greeleys in the stands. He patted Steve's shoulder as he sat down and thereafter had eyes only for the tennis.

Sure enough, Ginny easily won the match, six–one,

six–three. When she came over to accept the congratulations of her family, she was hardly breathing hard.

"Way to go, Gin," said Steve, exchanging low fives with her.

"Lookin' *tough!*" his mother chimed in.

"Very impressive, Ginny," said Vince.

Ginny turned bright red and stammered out her thanks. "Will you be able to see the finals?" she asked.

"I'll be there," replied Vince. "I look forward to watching both of Ted's kids. Ted, old buddy, you really turned out a couple of winners here."

Mr. Greeley grinned broadly.

Vince shook hands all around. "See you tomorrow," he said, as he turned and hurried away. Steve thought that Vince must spend a lot of his time rushing here and there.

"Yo, Steve!" Pat Carbo waved to him from the parking lot. "You all set?"

"Two minutes!" Steve said. He turned to his father. "Dad, I have to go. We'll talk about my game tonight, okay?"

His father frowned. "Hold on a minute, Champ. We were going to work on your serve-and-volley game for a while. I thought we'd find a practice court right now and —"

Steve stared in disbelief. "*Right now?* I just ran myself into the ground a little while ago, getting into the finals, Dad. This can wait till tomorrow." It was a rest day, before the finals.

His father shook his head. "It's better to concentrate on these problems while they're still fresh in your mind. I think we should do it *now.*"

Steve was hot and tired and decided that he wasn't going to give in. "Dad, I'm all played out today. I need a break. So I'm going to the mall with Pat for a while, all right? I'll see you at dinner, and you can give me your notes then, and we can work anytime tomorrow."

"But —," began Mr. Greeley.

Steve, however, had started running toward Pat. He grabbed Pat's arm, forcing him to run with him. He didn't slow up until they were out of sight of the tennis courts.

"Whoa!" said Pat, catching his breath. "What was

that all about? You just won a big match. How come your dad looked unhappy?"

Steve scowled. "He wanted me to go practice some stuff with him, but I said I was going with you. He didn't like it."

Pat whistled. "He wanted you to practice right after you'd played a long match? How come?"

"That's just how he is," Steve said. "Dad wants me to be a big tennis star. He wants me to go to a tennis camp for the summer that a friend of his runs, and I don't want to. I don't like the idea of doing nothing all summer but playing tennis, talking about tennis, and dreaming about tennis."

Pat thought about it for a minute. "Have you told him the way you feel?"

Steve sighed. "Nope. Not yet."

Pat stopped and turned to Steve. "Got any ideas on how and when you're going to do it?"

"Not a clue," answered Steve. "That's why I haven't done it yet."

Pat chewed on his lower lip, a sign that he was doing some heavy thinking. "You ought to tell him soon. The longer you wait, the harder it'll get."

Steve threw his hands out in frustration. "You

think I don't know that? I just . . . I wish I could . . . right now, I *can't*. That's all."

Pat studied his friend. "Just don't wait too long, or you may find yourself living out your Dad's plan and it'll be too late."

12

On the morning of the finals, Mr. Greeley announced another big surprise. He and Steve had worked out together the previous day and were at peace, for the moment.

"Want to know who'll be handing out your trophies today, after you win your titles?" he asked, sitting back and grinning at them.

"*If* we win," Steve corrected.

His father's smile disappeared. "I don't want to hear any negative thinking at this table."

Steve exchanged a quick look with Ginny, but Ginny seemed to side with their father on this one.

"The people presenting the trophies both worked with Vince, and he's going to introduce them to you," Mr. Greeley continued. "The boys' trophies will be handed out by . . . *Billy Gardiner!*"

Despite himself, Steve was impressed. Ginny squealed. *"Really? All right!"*

Billy Gardiner had begun his pro career twelve years ago, about when Steve was born. He was always ranked in the top twenty and had made it up to number two for a while. But though he'd won some tournaments, he'd never quite gotten to the top. Still, he was a big name in the sport.

"What about the girls' trophies?" asked Ginny.

"Dierdre Mulloy," Mr. Greeley replied.

"Dierdre Mulloy?" echoed Steve. "Didn't she retire?"

Ginny's eyes flashed angrily. "She definitely did *not* retire! She's making a comeback!"

Dierdre Mulloy had burst on the pro scene three years earlier, at the age of fourteen. For two years she had played, and often beaten, the best women on the tour. Then something had happened, and her game seemed to fall apart. She had dropped off the tour for several months but now, at seventeen, was back to see if she could recapture the magic.

"If there's time, Vince will introduce you to her before your match, Gin," said Mr. Greeley. "Later on, you'll both meet Billy. Of course," he added, putting down his coffee cup and looking at Steve as he spoke, "you'll be meeting them again — *when* they give you your trophies."

At the Tennis Center later that day, Steve and his parents were about to wish Ginny good luck when Vince came up with a tall young woman. Steve instantly recognized her as Dierdre Mulloy and knew from Ginny's muffled shriek that Ginny recognized her, too.

Dierdre was smiling, but the smile didn't reach her eyes. She seemed tense and kept looking everywhere except at the person she was talking to.

"It's a thrill to meet you," Ginny said.

Dierdre smiled, but not happily. "Well, at least you still recognize me, anyway."

Ginny stared in surprise. "*Recognize* you? Sure, I recognize you! You're a champ! *Everybody* recognizes you!"

Dierdre seemed to really look at Ginny for the first time. She sighed. "You'd think they would. I mean, it was only a year ago that I was on top, but . . . I'll bet a lot of people here don't know who I am."

Vince laughed. "Well, you'll be back on top soon, Dierdre. We know that much. It'll happen."

Dierdre nodded several times. "Sure. Absolutely. I . . . well, of *course* I'll be there! I *have* to be there." Steve felt a little uncomfortable at how desperate she sounded. He wondered why getting back on top was so important to her.

Vince put a hand on her arm. "Dee, don't worry. Just have some confidence. We're going to work everything out and you'll be right where you used to be."

She flashed him a grateful look. "I will, won't I? Because if I'm not — I — I guess I'd have to go back to school and — it would be — I couldn't just —"

She suddenly realized that the others were staring at her. Ginny looked astonished, and Steve was embarrassed.

Dierdre tried to laugh it off. "But I'm just being silly, and I'm looking forward to watching Ginny play — and to playing her on the tour someday!"

Vince gently took Dierdre's arm. "Save me a seat with you guys, will you? Dee and I are just going to talk for a moment."

As they walked away, Steve let out a long breath and said, "Yikes!"

Ginny whirled toward him. "What do you mean, 'yikes'? So she's kind of nervous and self-conscious. So what? She's been away for a while and she's rusty. She's still a great player!"

Steve held up his hands defensively. "Sure, Gin! I know that. I didn't mean — hey, you'd better get ready."

Ginny took off and the rest of the family sat down in the stands. Steve turned to his father. "Dierdre seemed real uptight, didn't she, Dad?"

Mr. Greeley looked thoughtful. "Well, when you've been to the top, it isn't easy thinking that you might not get back again, especially if you're still young."

So even if you're a champion, you can have a rough time, Steve thought as he settled into the stands to watch Ginny play. And this is what my dad really wants for me?

Ginny didn't look like her usual competitive self. She lost the first set of her match, six–four. But she quickly regained form and took the second and third sets by identical six–four scores.

Ginny came off the court as the fourteen-and-under state champion and was surrounded by her family. They all hugged her and showered her with praise. Then Vince stepped in.

"That was impressive, Ginny. The more I've seen of you, the more talent I think you've got. Maybe we can figure out a way for you *and* your brother to work with me in Florida."

He glanced at Steve, who made himself sound polite but not too eager.

Ginny's response came as a shock to Steve. She didn't jump up and down and scream. Instead she smiled and said, "Thanks, Mr. Marino. I really appreciate that. I'll talk it over with my folks. They may want me to wait a year."

Steve's jaw dropped. That sounded like something *he* might have said, pleasant but not exactly enthusiastic. Was Ginny feeling sick or something? He wished he could ask her what was going on, but he didn't think he'd be able to get her alone before he had to get ready for his own final. He was playing Tony Zaras, a guy who had beaten him a month before. He planned to take some time and think about how best to play Tony. Tony was the first seed — the highest ranked in the twelve-and-unders — this year, with reason.

Steve was just getting ready to leave when Vince waved someone over. Steve looked up to see Billy Gardiner standing in front of him.

As Vince made the introductions, Billy squeezed some kind of wrist-strengthening gizmo in his right hand. He put the thing in his pocket before shaking hands and then took it out and began squeezing again.

Steve pointed to the little device. "You use that every day?"

"You bet! Gotta keep the wrists strong," said Billy, never stopping his exercise.

"For how long?" asked Ginny.

Billy shrugged. "Dunno. A couple of hours, I guess. I don't keep track, I just do it. I also work out every day for four or five hours when I'm not play-ing. Young guys like Steve, here, are coming along all the time, and I have to stay in shape. If you don't work at it, you can lose it. I don't plan to lose it. But you have to put in your time at the gym and keep your edge."

"I remember when you competed in the French

Open," said Mr. Greeley. "That final was amazing. I thought for sure you were going to win."

Billy grinned broadly. "Hey, thanks."

Mrs. Greeley said, "I've always wanted to go to France. How did you like it?"

Billy thought a moment. "I play well on those red clay courts. It's my best surface."

Mrs. Greeley looked a little surprised. "No, I mean, how did you like the *country*? Did you travel, go to any of the museums, eat at any wonderful restaurants?"

"What's the view like from the top of the Eiffel Tower?" Ginny asked. "You've been all over the world; what country is your favorite?"

"Oh, I get you," said Billy, scratching his head. "I've never gotten to see too much in France, really. I go there to play tennis, so, you know, between practice and working out and watching videos of myself and getting my rest and watching the guys I might play to see how they look, I don't get to look around or do that kind of thing."

Billy grinned broadly. "And I always eat the same food, a special diet that I invented. I take a lot of the food with me, along with lots of vitamins and things.

So I don't have a chance to try local food. I guess I don't care too much about that other stuff, anyway. I'm just a tennis player."

"And a great one!" Mr. Greeley hastened to say. "You have any ideas what you're going to do when you retire from tennis?"

"Retire?" Billy stared as if the question was totally weird. "Oh, I don't think about that. First of all, I'm going to stay with the tour for another six or eight years. Then there's the senior tour. I'll stay in good shape so I'll play that till I'm sixty. Then maybe I'll retire — and keep playing for fun. Or maybe try to get a job on TV, doing analysis, interviews, something like that," he finished vaguely.

Steve and Ginny exchanged a look. Steve suddenly knew without a doubt that he didn't want his life to be like Billy Gardiner's. No way. There was too much else to enjoy, too many things he wanted to do.

Now all he had to do was make his dad listen to him. He had to.

13

Steve decided that Tony Zaras was the trickiest player he had ever faced. He decided this after he had fallen behind, three games to none, in the first set of the final. He was being driven crazy by Zaras's assortment of spins, slices, lobs, and drop shots, which had him back on his heels and confused. The same thing had happened, he remembered, when he had last played Tony a month before, and lost.

As he got ready to serve the fourth game, he tried to think of a way to turn this match around. He had to get back in control. Tony had weaknesses to be attacked. What were they?

There was Tony's backhand, for one thing. Tony used a two-handed grip. That made the backhand stronger, but it shortened his reach a little. Maybe Steve could concentrate more on the backhand, force him to run and lunge more, make Tony the guy who was off balance and uncertain for a change.

He tried the strategy on his next serve. Taking a deep breath, Steve sent a smash down the center-line, making Tony lunge at it with his two-handed backhand. As Steve had hoped, the return was weak, and he put away the point with a sizzling shot to the opposite corner.

Encouraged, Steve continued to use the same strategy for the rest of his serve. He was able to keep Tony from using his trick shots, and took the game.

But Tony came back to hold serve and still led, four games to one. While Steve successfully won his own service games for the rest of the set, Tony took the set, six games to three.

They continued to hold their serves in the second set, but it seemed to Steve that Tony was slowing down a little and having more trouble getting his breath. Steve continued to work on Tony's backhand and to make him run, from side to side and, with well-placed lobs, from net to baseline.

Uncharacteristically, Steve didn't charge the net at all until the second set score was four games apiece. He was watching Tony carefully. He thought he noticed that Tony had adjusted his play so that he could cover more of the court with his forehand.

On his next serve, Steve hit a ball that was slightly on Tony's backhand side. Sure enough, Tony side-stepped and made a forehand return — a slice that bounced away from Steve when it hit the surface. But Steve darted after the ball and returned a strong forehand. Tony hit it into the net for an unforced error. Steve won the game and led five games to four.

Okay, Steve thought. Time to pour on the juice.

Tony served to begin the next game. Steve slammed a fabulous return, then charged the net. Tony's hit sent the ball high and hard, right to Steve's outstretched racket. The ball flew back over the net so forcefully that Tony could only watch as it bounced high in the air out of his reach.

Tony's next serve was a topspin smash. Steve had to leap for it, but he hit it well. Both boys played the point from the baseline, until Tony hit a drop shot that was designed to bounce twice, softly, before Steve could reach it. Instead it bounced back on Tony's side. Tony was definitely tiring. Steve felt a surge of energy.

Tony tried another topspin serve, but Steve

gauged correctly where the ball would go after it bounced and hit a powerful return to Tony's forehand, in the corner of the court. Tony, expecting that Steve would hit to his backhand, was caught flat-footed and couldn't reach the ball. Steve now had three set points to work with.

Tony seemed rattled and served his first fault of the set. Steve moved in a little. When Tony's second serve proved soft, Steve hit it to his backhand, faked a charge toward the net, and then stopped short. Tony hit a lob, assuming that Steve would continue to the net. Steve was ready. He smashed another return out of Tony's reach to tie the match at one set apiece.

The crowd roared its approval.

As he prepared to serve the first game of the deciding set, Steve glanced at the stands where his family was sitting. Vince was with them, of course. A thought flashed across Steve's mind: If I lose this match, maybe Vince won't want me at the camp after all. That would solve his problem, for sure.

But he didn't want to lose. He wanted to *win*. Steve enjoyed playing tennis and always played to beat his opponent. If he lost, well, that was too bad, but it wouldn't ruin his life. Still, he liked winning better, and even though he didn't want tennis to become the only thing in his life — not now, not yet, and maybe never — he wanted to win this match and get that trophy.

And in order to get that trophy, he had to beat Tony Zaras. He turned his full attention back to his opponent.

Steve bounced the ball a few times. Then he tossed it up in the air and unleashed a beautiful top-spin serve that bounced crazily.

Tony's reflexes were sharp and he reached the ball but couldn't get much on it. Steve rocketed a backhand return across court to Tony's backhand. Tony netted it.

Steve went on to take the first game without Tony winning a point.

But Tony held his own serve. He won with his serve-and-volley game, coming to the net and punching the ball out of Steve's reach.

The next game was hard fought. Steve began his service with a powerful ace down the middle of the court that handcuffed Tony. But Tony's dazzling passing shot blew by Steve to make it fifteen-all.

Steve thought hard about what to do next . . . and

got so distracted he committed a foot fault, allowing part of his foot to go over the baseline before he hit his serve! Tony blasted Steve's second serve so hard that the ball hit the frame of Steve's racket. Tony was up, fifteen–thirty.

Steve lost his concentration and, two points later, the game. Tony had broken his serve.

But Steve bore down in the next game and came back to break Tony. The game winner came on a spectacular desperation dive, where Steve just got his racket on the ball and the ball just hit the baseline at the corner for an unreturnable winner. Two games each.

The two players moved to the side of the court before resuming play. Steve drank a little of the sports drink provided and wiped his hands, arms, and face with a towel. He took some slow, deep breaths, which his father had told him was a good way to stay calm and under control. He tried to block out the noise of the crowd.

But there was one thing he couldn't block out: the question of what he would say to his dad. He tried not to think of it, but it wouldn't go away. He sighed and got up to serve the fifth game. He looked up once more at his family. His dad gave him a big thumbs-up sign. Ginny waved and shouted something he couldn't hear.

Steve checked to see where Tony had positioned himself. Tony was edging away from the side of the court so he wouldn't have to cover as much area with his backhand. Steve decided to test that backhand anyway. He aimed toward the middle and hit the centerline with a nice, strong serve.

Tony's return kept Steve on the baseline. Steve sent the ball back to Tony's backhand side, moving in toward the net as he did so. But Tony hit a high lob that forced him to retreat.

He got to the ball in plenty of time. Once again, he aimed for Tony's backhand. He noted that when Tony hit his return, he stayed on the left side of the court instead of moving to the middle. Steve hit a hard smash to the right corner of the court. Tony just barely got to it with a lunge that left him off balance. Steve put his next shot out of reach.

Steve then served straight at Tony, who jerked to his left and hit an out-of-control forehand slice. The ball landed wide of the court. Steve led, thirty–love.

Tony took the next point, returning Steve's sloppy

serve with a beautiful passing shot straight down the line. Now Tony's rooters had their turn to cheer and shout encouragement.

Steve quieted them quickly. He served to Tony's backhand again, then moved to the net and hit a passing volley out of Tony's reach. It was forty–fifteen, and Steve decided to try to wear Tony down a little more.

Accordingly, he stayed back on the baseline and ran Tony back and forth from corner to corner. It was all Tony could do to make returns at all. He couldn't use any of his tricks, and he looked more and more tired.

Finally, when Tony started across court too soon in anticipation of a shot, Steve hit one behind him and won the game. He had the lead, three games to two.

Tony was able to hold his own serve, although each point was long and the game went to deuce five times before he put it away, evening up the final set at three games each. As soon as he won the game point, Tony bent over, hands on knees, breathing hard.

Steve thought to himself, I have to keep forcing him to run. He doesn't have as much energy in reserve as I do . . . I *hope*.

In the next game, Steve kept Tony on the defensive by forcing him to use his two-handed backhand a lot and making him run constantly. Steve knew that, at this point in the match, he *had* to hold his own serve.

Steve had the game at forty–love when he hit a ball too deep, giving Tony a point. Angry with himself for the unforced error, he lost concentration on the next point. Tony tipped a drop shot over the net for a winner, and suddenly it was forty–thirty.

Hoping to catch Tony by surprise for an ace, Steve hit his next serve to Tony's forehand side. But Tony managed to catch up to it and send the ball rocketing straight back. With a grunt of exertion, Steve stretched far to his right and made a clean return.

Tony hit cross-court, coming to the net as he did

so. Steve attempted a lob, but it wasn't high enough. Tony reached high and hit an overhand smash to Steve's left.

Steve dove and just got his racket on the ball. He skidded along the hard surface but made a decent return. He quickly rolled to his feet and sprinted across the baseline to return Tony's next volley. This time his lob was better and Tony had to back up to reach the ball. Steve tried a drop shot of his own. It ticked the top of the net and fell for game point. Steve led, four to three.

He set himself to receive Tony's serve, but the umpire called out, "Just a minute, please." Steve stared at him, puzzled.

The umpire leaned down from his chair and asked, "Are you all right, son?"

"Huh? What do you mean?"

"Look at your leg," suggested the umpire. "How do you feel?"

Steve looked down and saw blood running from a scrape on his left leg. He realized it must have happened on that last diving shot. He hadn't felt a thing, hadn't been aware of the scrape at all. Even now, he didn't feel much of anything.

"Are you all right?" the umpire repeated. "Can you go on?"

"Go on? *Sure!*" Steve replied. "Absolutely! I mean, I'm fine, it's nothing, just a little scrape."

The umpire nodded and studied Steve for a moment. "All right, then, but I think we should take a moment and clean it up."

Play was stopped and a tournament official appeared with a first aid kit. He cleaned the scrape and applied a disinfectant. Steve winced; *that* stung a little. The official then put a bandage on and patted Steve's shoulder.

"You sure you want to keep playing?" the umpire asked.

Steve was surprised. Who, he wondered, would default from a championship match on account of a little scratch? *He* definitely wouldn't, that's for sure.

But since the umpire seemed genuinely concerned, Steve flexed his knee to prove it was all right. And it was. The bandage restricted his movement a bit, but otherwise he felt normal.

"Definitely ready to play," Steve announced.

The umpire nodded. "Then let's go. The score is three games to four in the third set, Zaras to serve."

There was polite applause from the crowd in the stands.

Steve felt a slight twinge in the leg as he bounced in place, waiting for the serve. It came whizzing to his left. He sidestepped to reach it and felt the twinge again. His return was wide of the sideline.

"Out!" called the line judge. As he moved to the right side of the baseline, Steve blamed the break in play for messing up his concentration, not the scratch on his leg.

Tony missed on his first serve, hitting it into the net, and then hit a cautious second serve. Steve moved in and returned the ball straight down the line to Tony's backhand. Tony had to lunge for it. He put the ball right where Steve could smash a hard forehand down the line. Tony had to race to get the ball again, but he did manage to reach it.

Tony's return touched the tape on top of the net but bounced over. Steve had been running to make a backhand return, but the bounce off the tape gave the ball a crazy spin that sent it right to his knees. He put on the brakes and felt a stab of pain in the injured leg. Distracted, he failed to return the ball. Now he trailed, love–thirty.

Tony hit a beautiful topspin serve that Steve couldn't return. The ace brought the score to forty–love in Tony's favor. Steve managed to get one point, but Tony won the game, tying the set at four–four.

The crowd was now really into the match, yelling and cheering on every point, shouting encouragement to whichever boy they favored.

Steve found that his leg made a difference in his serve; he couldn't extend himself upward the way he usually did. On the first serve in the new game, he hit one into the net. On second service, he got it over but without much power, and Tony hit a slicing backhand return for a winner. Steve could imagine concern on his father's face in the stands.

He raised himself up on his toes a couple of times before the next serve. This time he hit it better — a hard shot to Tony's backhand. He was able to take control again. He moved Tony around, preventing the other player from setting himself and hitting his favorite shots. He won the next two points to lead, thirty–fifteen. Two more points and the game would be his.

With Tony edging over toward his backhand side,

Steve crossed him up by hitting it to his forehand. While Tony returned the ball, the shot didn't have much steam on it. Steve charged the net, hitting a volley past the diving Tony for a winner. Tony didn't get up for a moment. He was winded.

Steve wanted to end this game quickly and tried to freeze Tony by hitting the serve straight at him. But this time, Tony slid to his left and hit a hot cross-court forehand return. Steve went for it and hit it down the line. Tony got set for his two-handed backhand and sent it back to Steve's backhand side, running toward the net as he did.

Steve tried to pass Tony on Tony's left, but the other boy's reflexes were still sharp. He blocked the ball, sending it almost straight down on Steve's side of the net. Luckily, the ball took a high enough bounce for Steve to get to it. He tried once again to pass Tony. For a moment the boys faced each other from only a few yards away, both taking advantage of their quickness to make returns.

Then Steve hit a lob over Tony's head that Tony couldn't reach. Steve had won the game and led, five games to four. If Steve could break Tony's serve now, the match was his.

Tony was as much aware of this fact as Steve. He found some reserve energy somewhere, enough for him to take the game with the help of a couple of nice topspins.

That was probably Tony's best weapon, thought Steve, trying to loosen his leg a little. The scrape was becoming more and more of a problem to deal with.

The two players split the next two games, making the score six games apiece and setting up a tiebreaker to determine who would win the final match. Steve would serve the first point.

There was a brief break and the boys went to the side of the court. Steve decided to stay standing and flex his leg to make sure it didn't tighten up on him. Tony sat, breathing deeply and looking straight ahead. Then they took their places, to enthusiastic applause.

Steve served, down the middle, and stayed at the baseline. He didn't want to risk putting too much pressure on his leg. Tony hit a slicing return that forced Steve to lunge hard to his left to make a backhand return. It was out of reach. His leg was stiffening and sore enough to keep him from moving quickly from side to side. Could it cost him the match?

They switched sides for Tony's first tiebreaker serve. Steve continued to flex the leg, knowing that if it got any worse, he'd lose the match for sure.

Tony's serve came straight at him and he quickly sidestepped, slashing a forehand return to Tony's backhand side. Tony got to it and hit a return that ticked the net, forcing Steve to charge forward to make his shot. He gritted his teeth, resolving not to let the pain in his leg slow him down. He hit a passing shot down the right sideline. Tony started to dive for it but then let it go, undoubtedly hoping it would be wide. It wasn't, and the point was Steve's.

Tony's next serve was a perfect ace into the far corner of the service box, and he led, two–one.

Steve served to Tony's backhand and hit Tony's return to the opposite corner. Tony dashed to get it but mis-hit his shot. The ball dribbled off the edge of his racket. Two points each.

Steve took a deep breath and hit his best serve of the day, a rocket with plenty of spin that skidded away from Tony after just hitting the edge of the service box. He led, three–two.

Tony's next serve forced Steve to run to his left. Although he made the return, Steve felt pain in his leg as he reversed direction and headed back toward the middle of the baseline.

Tony clearly knew that Steve's leg was bothering him. He hit a drop shot that Steve had to charge to reach. He got there and stayed at the net. But Tony ripped a shot past him to tie the tiebreaker at three–three.

On the next point, the players got into a long baseline exchange. Neither wanted to come to the net: Tony looked to take advantage of Steve's leg problem, and Steve hoped to wear Tony down more by making him run. Finally, Tony came in and put away the point with a wicked, sliced volley that Steve couldn't reach. It was now four–three, with Tony in the lead.

Steve served next. He put some slice on the ball, which bounced away from Tony's racket. Tony stumbled a little and hit the ball into the net, and they were tied once again, at four–four.

On Steve's next serve he aimed straight at Tony. Once again, Tony froze for a fraction of a second and his return was soft and uncertain. Steve was able to take control and move Tony back and forth on the baseline again. Tony managed to get to the ball, but he was moving as if his feet were made of lead. Finally, Steve moved toward the net and volleyed the ball at such a sharp angle that Tony just stared at it. Steve led, five to four.

Tony now had two serves. Steve went in to meet the first one, only to see the ball squirt under his racket. Tony had put some slice on it and had come back to tie at five–five.

Steve's leg was throbbing and his mouth felt dry. He tried to ignore his body's distress signals and made a strong return of service down the center of the court, to Tony's backhand. Tony slammed a hard shot that was meant to pass Steve on his forehand side, but Steve's lunge was good enough for him to get the ball and send it steaming cross-court. Tony's return tipped the net. Steve had to throw himself forward to get his racket under the ball before its second bounce. The ball went softly over the net and Tony was unable to get there. Steve led, six–five. It was Steve's serve — and game, set, and match point.

As he walked back to serve, Steve was limping. He

couldn't try to hide the fact that his leg was aching, and he wanted this match to be over. If he didn't put Tony away right now, he would have a very rough time moving around with any speed.

He prepared to serve, barely aware of the cheering of the crowd in the stands. The umpire, however, called time.

"Quiet, please," he called out. "Please let the players concentrate." Once the crowd had settled down, the umpire signaled for Steve to serve.

Steve tossed the ball high, arched his back, and whipped his right arm around.

"*Out!*" called a line judge.

"Fault," said the umpire. "Second service."

Steve hesitated, bouncing the ball. Should he play it safe? Or should he go for broke and risk a double fault? He decided that he would have to take that risk, because he wasn't sure how much longer he'd be able to play on that leg. He figured he must have either a bad bruise or a slight strain. Either way, he wouldn't be able to keep running for long. He had to try to win the match on this serve.

He glanced at Tony. Tony had crept in a few feet, expecting Steve to play it safe. That decided it for

Steve. He hit a hard topspin serve into the outside corner of the service box. For a terrible second he thought it was long.

But it wasn't. The ball took a low bounce, just under Tony's racket. Ace!

"Game, set, and match to Greeley," called the umpire, but his voice was drowned out by the cheering of the crowd. Steve stood still for a moment and then limped to the net to shake hands with Tony.

Tony smiled as he shook hands. "Congratulations. You earned it today."

Steve smiled back. "You made me fight for every point. You're a tough man to beat."

As Steve came to the sideline, his father rushed up and threw his arms around him. "What a match!" he yelled. "You were amazing! Unbelievable! Wait'll you hear Vince! He wants you for his camp! He's totally sold on you!"

When his father mentioned Vince, Steve winced and bit his lip. Mr. Greeley noticed but didn't understand.

"That leg must really be hurting," he said. "But you played right through the pain! Talk about guts — you're a real competitor!"

Ginny rushed forward and hugged her brother.

"You did great! How's your leg?" She handed him a cold drink.

Steve took a deep swallow. "It's not too bad. I think I must've bruised it when I dove. It'll be real sore tomorrow, but . . . who cares?"

Brother and sister grinned at each other and laughed.

Ten minutes later, the umpire called out for quiet over the PA system. He then introduced Billy Gardiner, who presented the trophy for the State Junior Tennis Championship in the Boys' Twelve-and-Under Class to Steve. As Steve took the cup, Billy shook his hand and said, "I'm going to have to watch out for you in a few years, dude. You have what it takes."

Steve tried not to flinch when Billy shook his hand. All that exercise had given Billy a grip of steel. Billy grinned. "See you on the tour, kid."

Steve carried his trophy toward the locker room, accompanied by the rest of his family. Vince stood by the locker room door, smiling, his hand outstretched. "You really showed me something out there, Steve. How's the leg?"

Steve shrugged. "I don't think it's too bad. Maybe it's just a bruise."

"Be sure to ice it right away," Vince advised. "By the way, you and I have to talk this evening."

"This evening?" Steve echoed, suddenly feeling nervous.

Mr. Greeley said, "I guess I didn't mention it, but we're having a victory dinner tonight for you and Ginny, and Vince is the guest of honor. He has something to tell you both, something that'll make your day."

Steve hoped his feelings didn't show on his face. "Okay," he said. "Sure."

He ducked quickly into the locker room, not wanting to face his dad just yet. He put some ice in a towel and wrapped it around his sore leg. While he was letting the ice do its job, his buddy Pat came up and lightly punched his shoulder.

"You were awesome out there," he said. He noticed the wrapped leg. "You didn't break anything, did you?"

Steve shook his head. "Nothing like that. Just a bruise, I think."

Pat sat next to him. "You break the news to your dad yet? About your future?"

Steve didn't say anything. Pat looked concerned. "No, huh? When are you going to?"

Steve massaged the leg gently. "It has to be tonight, because I think Vince Marino is going to invite me officially to his camp. And I don't want to go. I'll have to tell dad before dinner, because I don't think he should hear the bad news for the first time when Vince invites me."

"Know what you're going to say?" asked Pat.

"I don't have a clue."

Pat stood up. "Oh, boy. Well, good luck. I wish I had some advice for you, but I don't have a clue either. Call me later and tell me how it went."

"Okay," Steve said. As Pat left, Steve shut his eyes and tried to relax. Suddenly he was aware that someone had sat down next to him. He was startled to see that it was Vince. He had taken off his mirrored sunglasses and was looking at Steve with a steady gaze.

"I thought you and I might have a little talk in private," Vince said. "I mean, without your dad around."

"Sure," said Steve, wondering what this was all about.

Vince sat back on the bench. "I already told you, Steve, you showed me something today. I don't just mean that you have good technique, either. You have that winning instinct, too.

"It would have been easy for you to just take it easy when that leg began to hurt. No one would have blamed you even if you'd said that you couldn't play anymore. After all, you're the only one who knew how bad you hurt. But you gutted it out. That meant more to me than your serve or your footwork."

"Thanks," Steve said, still not sure why Vince was telling him this without his father around to hear.

"But there's one thing I'm *not* sure about," Vince went on. "And I thought I'd bring it up just between you and me.

"See, I've worked with hundreds of tennis players. All of 'em were very good and a few were great, and while I've been teaching them, they've taught *me* a few things, too.

"The most important thing they taught me is that unless someone really *wants* to become a professional tennis player, it doesn't matter how much talent he or she has. All the teaching in the world isn't going to be enough. Are you following me?"

Steve shrugged. "Uh, sure. I follow you completely."

Vince nodded. "Good. Now, I get a feeling — I may be wrong, and correct me if I am — but I think you may not be wild about going to my camp. Am I right about that?"

Steve didn't know what to say. "Well, I mean, I know your camp is great and all, but . . ."

Vince smiled. "Don't worry about my feelings, just say what's on your mind. This is just between us. I won't tell your dad."

Steve was puzzled. "How could you tell?"

"Let's just say that I've learned to recognize the signs."

"But —" Steve stopped, trying to think things through. "If *you* can see, how come my dad can't?"

Vince sighed. "Don't be too hard on your dad, Steve. When he got hurt, back in college, it was almost like his life was over. Tennis had been the center of his life, and he probably would have had a good pro career. Then, *boom,* it was gone. Just like that." Vince shook his head sadly.

"Now here you are, his son, with the same kind of talent, and he naturally assumes you're going to want what *he* wanted back then. Can you under-stand why he would think that, and why it might not be easy for him to accept the fact that you don't feel the same way?"

"I guess," Steve answered. "Hey, maybe I *will* want to get serious about tennis someday. Maybe it'll happen next year, or the year after. I don't know. But —"

"But not just yet," Vince finished for him. "I get what you're saying. The thing is, you need to tell him."

Steve slumped, and then sat up hopefully. "Maybe you could tell him for me."

Vince shook his head again. "It should come from you. I know you don't want to do it, but you should tell him what's on your mind. It won't be so bad. Matter of fact, Ted may surprise you. In any case, you'll feel a lot better once you do."

Steve thought for a moment. "I guess you're right. Thanks. Thanks a lot."

Vince got up and patted Steve on the shoulder. "I'm glad we had our talk. See you tonight."

Steve sat there, wishing it were the next day and that the talk with his dad was history.

16

The victory dinner at the Greeleys that evening was not a huge success. Both Steve and Ginny were unusually quiet, which was surprising since both had won state championships that day. The Greeley parents and Vince kept the conversation flowing, but both Mr. and Mrs. Greeley kept giving their children looks of concern.

"Honey, are you feeling all right?" Mrs. Greeley finally asked Ginny.

"Sure, Mom, I'm fine," Ginny said, but not very convincingly.

"Leg bothering you, Champ?" Mr. Greeley asked Steve at another point.

"It's all right, Dad," replied Steve. "I iced it like Vince said and it's okay."

Finally, the dishes from the main course were cleared away and Mr. and Mrs. Greeley came out of the kitchen carrying a big layer cake with two candles on top. In the vanilla icing, big chocolate letters spelled out OUR TWO CHAMPIONS.

While the cake was being cut, Vince cleared his throat. "I guess this is a good time to tell you all my news. I'm happy to say that we have room for *both* of you at camp this summer, and from what I saw today, I'd like the chance to work with you, Ginny, and you, Steve."

Their father beamed in delight, though their mother looked less than happy.

"I thought that we —," she began, but Ginny interrupted her.

"Mom, it's okay. Mr. Marino —"

"You can call me Vince, remember?" he said.

"Okay," Ginny answered. "Vince, thanks a lot for inviting me but — I can't believe I'm saying this — but I don't think I should go."

Steve's jaw dropped. "*What?* But I figured . . . I was sure that you'd . . . how come, Gin?"

Ginny got up and hugged her mother. "Because

Mom is right. I need to work on my math. Tennis will have to wait."

"What changed your mind?" Mrs. Greeley asked.

"I guess it was listening to Dierdre Mulloy today. I mean, she's done everything I wanted to do, and she's really unhappy. If she can't make a comeback, she'll be unhappy for a long time. And I saw that it's partly because she doesn't know anything except tennis. Mom tried to explain that to me, but I guess until I met Dierdre, I wasn't ready to believe her."

"Dierdre may come back," Vince pointed out. "She's still a great athlete."

"Sure," Ginny agreed. "*Maybe.* And maybe not. I've been thinking a lot about it ever since this morning, and I decided I'd better take care of my education. If I work hard this school year, maybe I'd be able to come to your camp next summer, Vince — if you'd still let me, that is."

Vince said, "I don't see why not, if you want to come. You're still young and you're very good. And you also have a good head on your shoulders."

Mr. Greeley shrugged. "Well, that's that, then. Ginny will go to summer school, and Steve will go to Vince's camp."

"No, Dad." The words were out of Steve's mouth before he knew they were coming.

Mr. Greeley stared at his son. "What? Did you say no?"

Steve swallowed hard and nodded. "I feel the same way Gin does, Dad. I'm not . . . I'm not ready. Not yet, anyway."

"*Sure* you are!" his father replied. "You're as talented as any boy your age I've ever seen!"

"But I'm not *ready,*" Steve insisted, standing up and facing his father. "I know I have talent, and I like playing tennis, but . . . there are too many other things I want to do. I'm only twelve years old, and I don't want to spend my whole summer doing nothing but tennis."

His dad shook his head. "I can't believe what I'm hearing. Here you're getting the chance of a lifetime, and you're going to throw it away? Vince, help me out, here, will you? Tell the boy what he's ready to pass up!"

But Vince said, "Sorry, Ted, but I can't do that. This is between the two of you, and also . . . I don't think Steve is wrong."

Mr. Greeley opened his mouth, but no words

came out at first. "Vince, what are you saying?" he said finally. "You can't mean that. You just invited him to your camp, after all!"

"I *do* mean it," replied Vince. "Ted, you're a great judge of tennis ability. But only Steve knows what's going on inside his head. On that, he's the authority."

Mrs. Greeley gently put a hand on her husband's arm. "Dear, the fact is that Steve has been sending us signals that he wasn't sure what he wanted to do, but we didn't pick them up."

Ted looked bewildered. "I don't get it. You'd think I was being cruel and forcing Steve to do something awful, instead of setting him up for a great career."

"Dad, *you* met Billy Gardiner today," Steve jumped in. "You talked to him, you heard him. Nothing matters to him but tennis. He's traveled all over the world but never cared enough to look around. All he's ever done is tennis, and that's all he ever wants to do.

"Well, that's not *me*. I don't want to hurt your feelings and I'm sorry if I have, but I don't want to be another Billy Gardiner. Maybe I'll decide to get serious about tennis someday, and maybe I won't. I do

114

love playing, but there are other things that matter to me, too. Please don't be angry with me."

"*Angry?*" Mr. Greeley repeated, sitting down slowly. "Son, I'm not angry with you. I only thought that — I figured that you'd jump at this opportunity, that it would make you happy. I thought —"

He stopped suddenly. "You know what?" he said. "Maybe I didn't really *think* at all. I just assumed that you'd want what *I* always wanted. But, the fact is, I never actually asked you, did I? I guess I owe you an apology, son. I hope *you're* not angry at *me.*"

Steve ran over and hugged his father. "No way, Dad," he said. "I always knew you wanted what you figured was best for me. There's nothing to be angry at. But I had to tell you the way I felt."

Mr. Greeley hugged his son back and then looked at Ginny. "Honey, I owe you an apology. I had no idea tennis meant so much to you."

"I understand," Ginny said. "And I appreciate your saying that. And I'd appreciate it *more,*" she said, grinning, "if you'd give me pointers and work with me just like you do with Steve from now on."

"That's a deal," her father replied. "You could be a star someday — if you want to be, that is."

Vince slapped him on the back. "I had a hunch you'd react just like this. And I'll keep an eye on both your kids in the future. If they keep playing and want to work with me somewhere down the line, I think there will still be room for them."

"We still have something to celebrate," Mrs. Greeley reminded them. "And we have some delicious cake sitting here, begging to be eaten. Why don't we sit down and eat the cake as a tribute to our two champions? They're very special kids."

"Sounds good to me," Mr. Greeley said. "And it's not just their athletic talent that makes them great kids. They have brains, too."

"With parents like you two," said Steve, "it figures."

He took a forkful of cake.

Matt Christopher

Terrell Davis

John Elway

Julie Foudy

Wayne Gretzky

Ken Griffey Jr.

Mia Hamm

Grant Hill

Randy Johnson

Michael Jordan

Lisa Leslie

Tara Lipinski

Mark McGwire

Greg Maddux

Hakeem Olajuwon

Emmitt Smith

Sammy Sosa

Mo Vaughn

Tiger Woods

Steve Young

The #1
Sports Writer
for Kids

MATT CHRISTOPHER

Read them all!

- Baseball Flyhawk
- Baseball Pals
- Baseball Turnaround
- The Basket Counts
- Catch That Pass!
- Catcher with a Glass Arm
- Center Court Sting
- Challenge at Second Base
- The Comeback Challenge
- The Counterfeit Tackle
- Crackerjack Halfback
- The Diamond Champs
- Dirt Bike Racer
- Dirt Bike Runaway
- Double Play at Short

- Face-Off
- Fighting Tackle
- Football Fugitive
- The Fox Steals Home
- The Great Quarterback Switch
- The Hockey Machine
- Ice Magic
- Johnny Long Legs
- The Kid Who Only Hit Homers
- Long-Arm Quarterback
- Long Shot for Paul
- Long Stretch at First Base
- Look Who's Playing First Base
- Miracle at the Plate
- Mountain Bike Mania

All available in paperback from Little, Brown and Company